A Walk with Henrietta

Words by: Amanda Esch-Cormier

Illustrations by: Julian Fransci

ISBN
978-1-7378393-3-0

Library of Congress: 2022914011

To Dad,
Thanks for sharing your love of the outdoors.

"All summer?" I shouted.

"We have to be here all summer?"

I looked around at Uncle's farm. It was so BORING here. There was nothing to do, and no kids to play with. And everything was so old!

Mom gave me those eyes she's so good at.

"Yes, all summer. And I think you'll find it's not so boring at all. Why don't you take Izzy and go explore."

I rolled my eyes at Mom, but there was nothing better to do, so I put on Izzy's leash, and the two of us set off.

I'd never explored a place like this. It was so different from the cement city blocks of home.

The morning dew was still glistening on the grass as I made my way along the path. I giggled as it slipped between my toes.
The water tickled, like the grass was giving my feet a bath.

"Look Izzy," I whispered. "A doe!"

"Hey, Mama" I said, as I often did to animals we passed by.

I watched the doe, and she watched me back.

I expected for her to get scared and run off into the brush, but she didn't seem afraid.

The leash fluttered in my hand. I knew Izzy wanted to chase her, but she stayed calm and still.

"Good girl," I said. "Come on. Let's leave her be."

Turning, I saw that the doe was following us. I couldn't believe it. I'd always heard deer were easily scared. But this one didn't seem that way at all. She seemed gentle . . . and interested. Like she wanted to be my friend.

More than anything, I wanted to be her friend, too. But how could I do that? Then I knew. I'd talk to her!

"The sun sure is beautiful today, isn't it?" I asked her. "Do you like the flowers at the top of the hill? Which ones are your favorite?"

"At each of my questions, she nodded and sniffed, as if she understood what was being said. I giggled as she bobbed her head up and down like she was doing a dance. I wondered what music she heard to make her move that way.

"Do you have a name?" I asked, but she remained still and silent.
"Do you want one?" I asked.
At that, she flicked her head, which I took to mean yes.
"Penny?" She snorted, and I took that as a no.
"Abigail?" She snorted again.
"Hmmm . . . Henrietta?"
The doe looked up quickly.
"Henrietta it is," I said.

The three of us turned to walk along the river. The field was open here. I worried that someone else from the farm would see us and call out, scaring her away. But unlike any other day here, we didn't see anyone, and our friend Henrietta kept walking stride for stride with us.

"What is it like living here on the farm? Do you meet a lot of people?" I asked. The farm didn't feel like the right place for me, but it did seem like a nice place for a deer.

As we approached the pasture, Henrietta stopped at the fence.

She greeted some of the sheep with the same sniffing and head bobbing she'd used to respond to me.

I said hello to the sheep, too, but their focus was on Henrietta.

"Come on, Henrietta. We're going to head up the hill. Mom says sheep are scared of us."
I turned to make my way toward the hill, but Henrietta stayed at the fence, greeting the sheep one by one.

Watching this greeting of old friends, I knew this was where we'd leave her.

My eyes locked with Henrietta's. She nodded her head to me, as if to say goodbye.

"Bye, Henrietta," I said.

"I hope we see you again soon. Thank you for walking with us today. It really made my morning better."

Then Izzy and I walked up the hill, leaving Henrietta behind with the sheep.

A few mornings later, Izzy and I went looking for Henrietta, but we couldn't find her.
All summer we tried, but Henrietta never crossed our path again.

I sometimes wonder if she was like me that day. Maybe the farm wasn't really her home, either, but we found each other on a day we both needed a new friend.

Either way, I hope I touched her life, just like she touched mine!

CPSIA information can be obtained
at www.ICGtesting.com
Printed in the USA
LVHW071408300822
727187LV00001B/8